KV-372-185

WALTER TULL AND THE MISSING FOOTBALL

by Damian Harvey and Claudia Marianno

W
FRANKLIN WATTS
LONDON•SYDNEY

Grandad was born in 1907.

That was before the First World War.

This is a picture of Grandad playing football when he was little.

COVENTRY CITY LIBRARIES

3 8002 02620 682 3

Grandad loved football. One day I asked him who his favourite player was.

"Walter Tull," said Grandad.

"Who is that?" I asked.

"Walter Tull was a great man," said Grandad. "I even met him once."

Then Grandad told me all about Walter Tull.

Walter Tull was born in Folkstone, Kent in 1888. His mother was from Folkstone, but his father was from Barbados, in the Caribbean.
Walter and his older brother, Edward, were happy living in Folkstone.

But when Walter was only seven years old,
his mother died. His father died just
two years later. After that, Walter and
his brother were sent to live in a
children's home in East London.
Edward was later adopted by a family
in Scotland. Poor Walter was left on his own.

5

Walter was good at playing football.
"When he grew up, he played for Clapton,
his local team. He even helped them win
three cups," said Grandad.

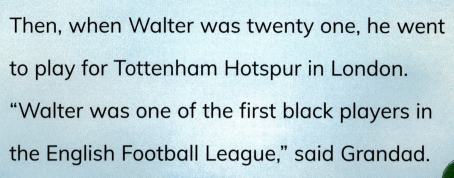

Then, when Walter was twenty one, he went to play for Tottenham Hotspur in London. "Walter was one of the first black players in the English Football League," said Grandad.

Some of the fans were rude to Walter because he was black.

"I don't want to stay here," said Walter.

"I'm going to play for another team."

So, in 1911, he left London and went to Northampton. He played more than a hundred games for Northampton Town.

But in August 1914, the First World War began.

Walter stopped playing football and decided

to become a soldier.

"I want to fight for my country," he said.

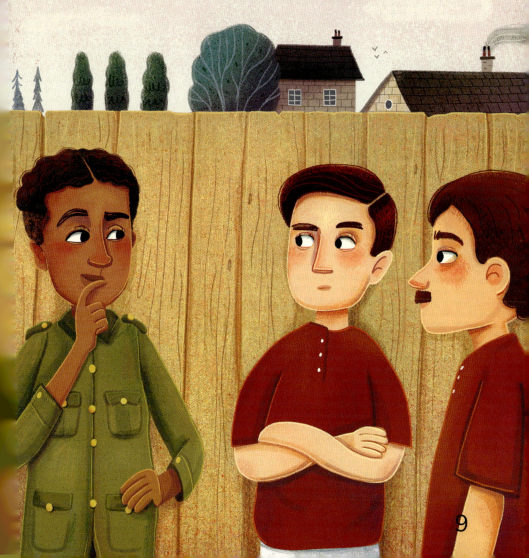

Walter travelled to London and joined the Footballers' Battalion. While they were training, the footballers could go home and play for their teams. Walter's team played near Grandad's home.

One day, when Grandad was still a boy,

he watched Walter and his friends

playing football. They were having fun

until the ball went into a field.

"We've lost our ball," said Walter.

"I'll help you look for it," said Grandad.

But they couldn't find the ball anywhere.

The next day, Grandad went back to have another look for the lost ball.

"I've found it," he cried. "Now I need to find Walter Tull."

Grandad waited near the army camp until some wagons drove out. He could see Walter in the first wagon.

"Stop!' shouted Grandad. "I found your ball. It was hidden in the long grass."

Walter jumped down. He looked very smart in his uniform. "Thanks," he said. "I'll take it to France with me. We might get a game against the other side."

13

In France, Walter and his battalion fought the enemy in miles of muddy trenches. He fought in the Battle of the Somme and in Northern Italy. Walter was brave and the other men trusted him.

In 1917, Walter became an officer.

"He was the first black officer in

the British Army," Grandad told me.

On New Year's Day 1918, Walter led his men on a daring mission.

"Follow me!" said Walter. "We have to cross this river." Walter led them across the icy river, and then safely back again.

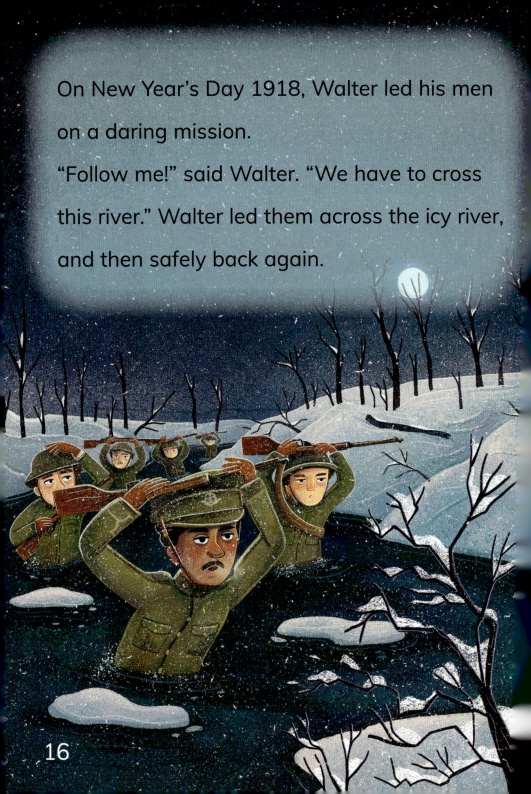

Because of his bravery, some people wanted Walter to be given the military cross.

Sadly, he never received it.

In March 1918, while he was leading his men into battle, Walter was killed.

Daily Express

LATE EDITION

ENGLAND 15 MARCH, 1918

WALTER TULL KILLED IN BATTLE

Then Grandad showed me a picture of some soldiers playing football.

"It was Christmas Day," said Grandad. "They stopped fighting and put down their guns. Then they played football together."

"Is that Walter's ball?" I asked.

Grandad smiled. "I like to think so," he said.

"Walter Tull was a good and brave man," said Grandad. "And that's why he is my favourite footballer. He is someone that we should never forget."

Story order

Look at these 5 pictures and captions.
Put the pictures in the right order
to retell the story.

1

Walter joins the army.

2

Walter loses a football in the field.

3

Grandad has a picture of soldiers playing football.

4

Walter wins many football trophies.

5

Grandad returns the football to Walter Tull.

Independent Reading

This series is designed to provide an opportunity for your child to read on their own. These notes are written for you to help your child choose a book and to read it independently.

In school, your child's teacher will often be using reading books which have been banded to support the process of learning to read. Use the book band colour your child is reading in school to help you make a good choice. *Walter Tull and the Missing Football* is a good choice for children reading at White Band in their classroom to read independently. The aim of independent reading is to read this book with ease, so that your child enjoys the story and relates it to their own experiences.

About the book

This is a fictional story about a grandad telling his grandson about meeting Walter Tull. The biographical details of Walter Tull are based on real events in history. Walter Tull (1888–1918) was one of the first black professional footballers before becoming the first ever black officer in the British army. He was killed in battle during the First World War.

Before reading

Help your child to learn how to make good choices by asking: "Why did you choose this book? Why do you think you will enjoy it?" Ask your child if they know anything about Walter Tull. Explain that this story links to real events in history. Then look at the cover with your child and ask: "What might happen in this story? What sort of clothing is Walter Tull dressed in?" Remind your child that they can break words into groups of syllables or sound out letters to make a word if they get stuck. Decide together whether your child will read the story independently or read it aloud to you.

During reading

Remind your child of what they know and what they can do independently. If reading aloud, support your child if they hesitate or ask for help by telling them the word. If reading to themselves, remind your child that they can come and ask for your help if stuck.

After reading

Support comprehension by asking your child to tell you about the story. Use the story order puzzle to encourage your child to retell the story in the right sequence, in their own words. The correct sequence can be found on the next page. Help your child think about the messages in the book that go beyond the story and ask: "Why did Grandad want to tell his Grandson about Walter Tull? Why do you think Grandad wanted to return the missing football to Walter? What would you do if you found something that someone had lost? Give your child a chance to respond to the story: "Did you have a favourite part? Why do you think Walter decided to join the army? How would you describe Walter's character?"

Extending learning

Help your child predict other possible outcomes of the story by asking: "What do you think would have happened if Walter had not joined the army? Or if Grandad had not met Walter Tull?" In the classroom, your child's teacher may be teaching how to look for evidence in texts to build opinions of characters. The story contains examples you can look at together such as: 'Walter was brave and other men trusted him', 'I want to fight for my country'. Discuss what impression these phrases give of Walter's character. Look for other examples in the text.

Franklin Watts
First published in Great Britain in 2024
by Hodder and Stoughton

Copyright © Hodder and Stoughton Ltd, 2024

Series Editors: Jackie Hamley and Melanie Palmer
Series Advisors and Development Editors: Dr Sue Bodman and Glen Franklin
Series Designers: Cathryn Gilbert and Peter Scoulding

A CIP catalogue record for this book is
available from the British Library.

ISBN 978 1 4451 8896 6 (hbk)
ISBN 978 1 4451 8897 3 (pbk)
ISBN 978 1 4451 9518 6 (ebook)

Printed in China

Franklin Watts
An imprint of
Hachette Children's Group
Part of Hodder and Stoughton
Carmelite House
50 Victoria Embankment
London EC4Y 0DZ

An Hachette UK Company
www.hachette.co.uk

www.reading-champion.co.uk

FSC
www.fsc.org
MIX
Paper | Supporting
responsible forestry
FSC® C104740

Answer to story order: 4, 1, 2, 5, 3